The Secret Princess

and other princess stories

Compiled by Tig Thomas

Miles Kelly

First published in 2013 by Miles Kelly Publishing Ltd
Harding's Barn, Bardfield End Green, Thaxted, Essex, CM6 3PX, UK

2 4 6 8 10 9 7 5 3 1

Publishing Director Belinda Gallagher
Creative Director Jo Cowan
Editorial Director Rosie McGuire
Senior Editor Claire Philip
Senior Designer Joe Jones
Production Manager Elizabeth Collins
Reprographics Stephan Davis, Jennifer Hunt, Thom Allaway

ISBN 978-1-78209-217-9

Printed in China

British Library Cataloguing-in-Publication Data
A catalogue record for this book is available from the British Library

ACKNOWLEDGEMENTS
The publishers would like to thank the following artists who have contributed to this book:
Smiljana Coh, Mélanie Florian, Kirsten Wilson, Jennie Poh, Karen Sapp (cover)

All other artwork from the Miles Kelly Artwork Bank

The publishers would like to thank the following sources for the use of their photographs:
Cover frame: Karina Bakalyan/Shutterstock.com
Inside frame: asmjp/Shutterstock.com

Made with paper from a sustainable forest
www.mileskelly.net   info@mileskelly.net

Contents

The Shepherdess

By Paul Sébillot

ONCE UPON A TIME there lived a king who had two daughters. He loved them both very much. When they grew up, he made up his mind that he would give his kingdom to the one who could best show how much she loved him.

So he called the eldest princess and said to her, "How much do you love me?"

"You are the apple of my eye," she said.

"Ah!" exclaimed the king, "you are indeed a good daughter."

Then he sent for the younger daughter, and asked her how much she loved him.

"I love you, my father," she answered, "as I love the salt in my food."

This made the king very angry for salt seemed a very little thing to him, and he ordered her to leave the court, and never appear before him again. The poor princess made a bundle of her jewels and her best dresses and hurriedly left the castle where she was born.

She walked away, without knowing what was to become of her, for she had never been shown how to work. And as she was afraid that no one would want to hire a girl with such a pretty face, she decided to make herself as ugly as she could.

She took off her royal dress and put on some horrible old rags belonging to a

beggar. After that she
smeared mud all over
her hands and face,
and shook her hair into
a great tangle. After
walking for a great many
days she came to a
neighbouring kingdom. She
arrived at a large farm where
they needed a shepherdess, and
were glad to hire her.

One day when she was watching her
sheep in a lonely part of the country, she
felt a wish to dress herself in her robes of
splendour. She washed herself in the stream
and put on her fine robes, which she always
carried with her. The king's son, who had
lost his way out hunting, saw her from a
distance, and wished to look at her closer.

The Shepherdess

But the girl sped into the wood as swiftly as a bird. When she was quite safe, she put on her rags again, and smeared mud over her face and hands. However the young prince, who was both hot and thirsty, found his way to the farm to ask for a drink, and he asked the name of the beautiful lady that looked after the sheep.

At this everyone began to laugh, for they said that the shepherdess was one of the ugliest and dirtiest creatures under the sun.

The prince thought some witchcraft must be at work, and he went away before the return of the shepherdess.

But the prince thought often of the lovely maiden. At last he dreamed of nothing else, and grew thinner day by day until his parents promised to do all they could to make him as happy as he once was. He dared not tell them the truth, so he only said that he should like some bread baked by the shepherdess from the distant farm.

The maiden showed no surprise at receiving such an order, but merely asked for some flour, salt and water. Before beginning her work she washed herself carefully, and even put on her rings. While she was baking, one of her rings slid into the dough. When she had finished she dirtied herself again so that she became as ugly as before.

The loaf was brought to the king's son, who ate it with pleasure. But in it he found the ring of the princess, and declared to his parents that he would marry the girl whose finger that ring fitted.

So the king made a proclamation through his whole kingdom and ladies came from afar to win the prince. But the ring was so tiny that even those who had the smallest hands could only get it on their little fingers. In a short time all the maidens of the kingdom had tried on the ring. The king was just about to announce that their efforts had been in vain, when the prince said he had not yet

seen the shepherdess. They sent for her, and she arrived covered with rags, but with her hands cleaner than usual, so that she could easily slip on the ring.

The king's son declared that this was the girl he would marry. When his parents remarked that the girl was only a keeper of sheep the maiden said that she was born a princess, and that, if they would give her some water and leave her alone in a room for a few minutes, she would show them. They did what she asked, and when she entered in a magnificent dress, she looked so beautiful that all believed her. The king's son asked if she would marry him. The princess then told her story, and asked to invite her father to the wedding.

It was with great joy that the princess's father heard that she was alive and that a prince asked her hand in marriage. He had been deeply sorry for his hard words to her, and he hurried to be at the ceremony.

At the wedding feast they served her father bread without salt, and meat without seasoning. Seeing him eat very little, his daughter asked if he liked his food.

"No," he replied, "the dishes are carefully cooked, but they are all so tasteless."

"Did I not tell you, my father, that salt was the best thing in life?"

The king hugged his daughter, and begged her forgiveness. Then, for the rest of the wedding feast they gave him bread made with salt, and dishes with seasoning, and he said they were the best he had ever eaten.

The Mother and the Daughter who Worshipped the Sun

By Flora Annie Steele

ONCE UPON A TIME there lived a mother and a daughter who worshipped the Sun. Though they were very poor, they never forgot to honour the Sun, giving everything they earned to it except two small cornmeal cakes — one of which the mother ate, while the other was the daughter's share. Every day one cake apiece, and that was all.

Now it so happened that one day, when the mother was out at work, the daughter grew hungry, and ate her cake before dinnertime. Just as she had finished it a priest came by, and begged for some bread. So the daughter broke off half of her mother's piece and gave it to the priest in the name of the Sun.

By and by the mother returned, very hungry for her dinner, and lo and behold there was only half a cake left.

"Where is the remainder of the bread?" she asked.

"I ate my share of the cake," said the daughter, "and just as I finished, a priest came begging, so I was obliged to give him your half."

"A fine story!" said the mother, in a rage.

The Mother and the Daughter who Worshipped the Sun

"I believe you gave my cake in order to save yours!"

The daughter protested that she really had finished her cake before the priest came begging. She promised to give her mother her share the next day. But her mother told her to leave home, saying, "I will have no greedyguts in my house!"

So the daughter wandered away into the wild, crying. When she had gone a long, long way, she became very tired and climbed into a pipal tree for safety. She still cried while she rested among the branches.

After a time, a young prince came to the tree and lay down to sleep. As he lay there, he looked so beautiful. The daughter could not keep her eyes

The Mother and the Daughter who Worshipped the Sun

off him, and so her tears flowed down onto him like a summer shower upon the young man's face. He woke with a start. Thinking it was raining, he rose to look at the sky, and see where this sudden storm had come from, but far and near not a cloud was to be seen. So he swung himself into the tree, and lo and behold, he found a beautiful maiden sitting in the tree, weeping sadly.

The Mother and the Daughter who Worshipped the Sun

"Where do you come from, fair stranger?" said he, and with tears in her eyes she told him she was homeless and motherless. He fell in love with her sweet face and soft words, so he asked her to be his bride, and she went with him to the palace, her heart full of gratitude to the Sun, who had sent her such good luck.

Everything she could desire was hers, but when the other women talked of their homes she held her tongue, for she was ashamed of hers.

Everyone thought she must be some great princess, she was so lovely and magnificent, but in her heart of hearts she knew she was nothing of the kind, so every day she prayed to the Sun that her mother might not find her out.

But one day, when she was sitting alone

in her beautiful palace, her mother appeared, ragged and poor as ever. She had heard of her daughter's good fortune, and had come to share it.

"And you shall share it," pleaded her daughter. "I will give you back far more than I ever took from you, if only you will not disgrace me before my prince."

"Ungrateful creature!" stormed the mother, "did you forget that it was through my act that your good fortune came to you? If I had not sent you out into the world, where would you have found so fine a husband?"

"I might have starved!" wept the daughter, "and now you come to destroy me again. Oh great Sun, help me now!"

Just then the prince came to the door, and the poor daughter was ready to die of shame and vexation, but when she turned to where her mother had sat, there was a magnificent golden stool.

"My princess," asked the prince, astonished, "where does that golden stool come from?"

"From my mother's house," replied the daughter, full of gratitude to the great Sun, who had saved her from disgrace.

"If there are such wonderful things to be seen in your mother's house," said the prince, "I must go and see it. Tomorrow we will set out on our journey, and you shall show me all it contains."

In vain the daughter put forward one excuse after another. The prince's curiosity had been aroused by the sight of the marvellous golden stool, and he was not to be put off.

Then the daughter cried once more to the great Sun, in her distress, saying, "Oh gracious Sun, help me now!"

But no answer came, and with a heavy heart she set out the next day to show the prince her mother's house. A fine procession they made, with horsemen and footmen clothed in royal liveries surrounding the coach, where the daughter sat, her heart sinking at every step.

And when they came close to where her mother's hut used to stand, there on the horizon was a shining, flaming golden palace that glittered and shone like solid sunshine. Within and without all was gold. A golden mother came out to greet them. She spoke graciously, for she remembered nothing about her trip to the prince's palace!

There they stayed, admiring the countless

marvels of the Sun palace for three days, and when the third day was over, the prince, more in love with his bride than ever, turned homewards. But when he came to the spot where he had first seen the glittering golden palace from afar, he thought he would take just one more look at the wondrous sight,

and lo, there was nothing to be seen except a low thatched hovel!

He turned to his bride, full of anger, and said, "You are a witch, and have tricked me! Confess, if you would not have me strike you dead!"

But the daughter fell on her knees, saying, "My gracious prince, believe me, I have done nothing! I am a poor homeless girl. I prayed to the Sun, and the Sun helped me!"

Then she told the whole story from beginning to end, and the prince was so well pleased that from that day he too worshipped the Sun.

The Secret Princess

A traditional Russian fairy tale

ONCE UPON A TIME there was a prince and princess who lived happily together. They loved each other very much and had nothing to worry them, but at last the prince grew restless. He longed to go out into the world to try his strength in battle against some enemy and win all kinds of honour.

So he called his army together and gave orders to start for a distant country where there ruled a cruel prince who ill-treated his subjects. The prince said goodbye to his beloved wife, and set off with his army across the seas.

I cannot say whether the voyage was short or long, but at last he reached the country and marched on, defeating all who came in his way. But this did not last long, for in time he came to a mountain pass, where a large army was waiting to take the prince himself prisoner.

He was captured easily, and carried off to prison and now our poor friend had a very bad time indeed. All night long the prisoners were chained up, and in the morning they were yoked together like oxen and had to plough the land till it grew dark. It was a miserable place.

This state of things went on for three years before the prince found any means of sending news of himself to his dear princess, but at last he managed to send this letter:

> Sell all our castles and palaces, and then come and deliver me out of this horrible prison.

The princess received the letter, read it, and wept bitterly as she said to herself, "How can I rescue my dearest husband?"

She thought, and at last an idea came to her. She cut off all her beautiful long brown hair and dressed herself in boy's clothes. Then she took her lute and went forth into the wide world. The princess travelled through many lands before she got to the town where the bad prince lived. When she got there she walked all round the palace and at the back she saw the prison.

Then she went into the great court in front of the palace, and taking her lute in her hand, began to play and sing as beautifully as she could.

When the cruel prince heard this touching song, sung by such a lovely voice, he had the singer brought before him.

"Welcome, O lute player," said he. "Where do you come from?"

"My country, sire, is far away across many seas," said the princess, "For years

I have been wandering about the world and gaining my living by my music."

The wicked prince replied, "Stay here a few days, and when you wish to leave I will give you what you ask for in your song — your heart's desire."

So the lute player stayed on in the palace and sang and played almost all day long to the prince.

After three days the lute player came to say goodbye to the prince.

"Well," said the prince, "what do you want as your reward?"

"Sire, give me one of your prisoners," she replied, "You have so many in your prison, and I should be glad of a companion on my journeys. When I hear his happy voice as I travel along I shall think of you."

"Come along then," said the prince,

"choose who you want." And he took the lute player through the prison himself.

The princess picked out her husband and although the cruel prince was not happy with her choice, she took him with her on her journey. Their journey lasted a great many days, but he never found out who she was, although he asked many times. Instead, the secret princess led him nearer to his own country.

When they reached the frontier the prisoner said, "Let me go now, kind lad. I am no common prisoner, but the prince of this country. Let me go free and ask what you will as your reward."

"Do not speak of reward now," said the lute player. "Go in peace." And so they parted ways. The princess took a short way home, got there before the prince and changed her dress. An hour later all the people in the palace were running to and fro and crying out with great excitement, "Our prince has come back! Our prince has returned to us!"

The prince greeted everyone kindly, but he would not so much as look at the princess. Then he called all his council and ministers together and said to them, "See what sort of a wife I have. She is happy to see me, but when I was pining in prison, she did nothing to help me."

And his council had to agree — they answered, "Sire, when news was brought from you the princess disappeared and no one knew where she went. She only returned to us today."

The prince was very angry indeed with the princess. He cried, "Why, you would never have seen me again, if a young lute player had not rescued me. I shall remember him with gratitude as long as I live."

Whilst the prince was sitting with his council, the princess put on her travelling cloak to disguise herself again. She took her lute, and slipping into the court sang, clear and sweet.

As soon as the prince heard this song he ran out to meet the lute player, took him by the hand and led him into the palace.

"Here," he cried, "is the boy who released me from my prison. And now, my true friend, ask for anything and I will give you your heart's desire."

"Sir, I ask of you what I asked and got from the bad prince. But this time I don't mean to give up what I get. I want you!"

And as she spoke she threw off her cloak

and everyone saw it was the princess.

Who can tell how happy the prince was? He held a great feast for his whole kingdom, and everyone came and rejoiced with him for a week. I was there too, and ate and drank many good things. I shall not forget it as long as I live.

The Twelve Huntsmen

A traditional Spanish fairy tale

ONCE UPON A TIME there was a prince who was engaged to a princess whom he dearly loved. One day as he sat by her side feeling very happy, he received news that his father was lying at the point of death, and wanted to see him before his end.

So he said to his love, "Alas! I must go off and leave you, but take this ring and wear it as a remembrance of me, and when I am king I will return and fetch you home."

Then he rode off, and when he reached his father he found him very near death.

The sick king said, "Dearest son, I have wanted to see you again before my end. Promise me, I beg of you, that you will marry who I choose," and he then named the daughter of a nearby king. The prince was so sad that he could think of nothing but his father, and cried, "Yes, yes, dear father, whatever you desire shall be done." And then the king closed his eyes and died.

After the prince had been proclaimed king, he felt that he must keep the promise he had made to his father, so he sent to ask for the hand of the king's daughter, which was granted to him.

Now, his first love heard of this, and the thought of her lover's desertion made her so sad that she pined away and nearly died.

Her father said to her, "My dearest child, why are you so unhappy? If there is anything you wish for, say so, and you shall have it."

His daughter thought for a moment, and then said, "Dear father, I wish for eleven girls as near as possible to my height, age and appearance."

So the king had his kingdom searched till eleven maidens of the same height, age and appearance as his daughter were found and brought to the palace.

Then the princess asked for twelve complete huntsmen's suits to be made, all exactly alike, and the eleven maidens had to dress themselves in eleven of the suits, while she herself put on the twelfth.

After this she said goodbye to her father, and rode off with her girls to the court of her former love. Here she enquired whether the king wanted some huntsmen, and if he would not take them all as his servants. The king saw her but did not recognize her, and said he would gladly hire them all. So they became the royal huntsmen.

Now, the king had a most remarkable lion, for it knew every hidden secret. One evening the lion said to the king, "You think you have got twelve huntsmen?"

"Yes, certainly," said the king.

"There you are mistaken," said the lion, "they are twelve maidens."

"That cannot possibly be," replied the king, "how do you mean to prove that?"

"Just have a number of dried peas scattered over the floor of your chamber," said the lion, "and you will soon see. Men have a strong, firm tread, so that if they happen to walk over peas not one will stir, but girls trip and slip and slide, so that the peas roll all about."

Fortunately one of the king's servants had become very fond of the young huntsmen, and he went to them and said, "The lion wants to persuade the king that you are only girls," and he told them all the plot.

The princess thanked him, and after he was gone she said to her maidens, "Make every effort to tread firmly on the peas."

Next morning, when the king sent for his twelve huntsmen, and they passed through the chamber — which was plentifully strewn with peas — they trod so firmly and walked with such a steady step that not one pea moved. After they were gone the king said to the lion, "There now — you have been telling lies — you see they walk like men."

"Because they knew they were being put to the test," answered the lion, "and so they made an effort. Have a dozen spinning-wheels placed in the chamber. When they pass through you'll see how interested they will be, quite unlike any man."

But the good-natured servant went to the huntsmen and told them this fresh plot. Then, as soon as the princess was alone with her maidens, she exclaimed, "Now, make sure you don't even look at those spinning-wheels."

When the king sent for his twelve huntsmen next morning they walked through the chamber without even casting a glance at the spinning-wheels.

The king said once more to the lion, "Why, you have deceived me again — they are men, for they never once looked at the spinning-wheels."

So the twelve huntsmen continued to follow the king, and he grew daily fonder of them. One day whilst they were all out hunting the news was brought that the king's intended bride was on her way.

When the true bride heard of this she felt as though a knife had pierced her heart, and she fell fainting to the ground. The king ran up to help, and began drawing off his gloves. Then he saw the ring that he had given to his first love, and as he gazed into her face he knew her again. His heart was so touched that he kissed her, and as she opened her eyes, he cried, "I am yours and you

are mine, and there is no power on earth that can alter that."

To the other princess he sent a messenger to beg her to return to her own kingdom. "For," said he, "I have a wife, and he who finds an old key does not need a new one."

And so the wedding was celebrated with great joy, and the lion was the chief guest, for after all he had told the truth.